PU

Magic Take Off

Toby Forward was born in Coventry. He went to college to pursue theological training and subsequently became a parish priest. He is now a full-time writer and lives with his wife and two daughters near Hull.

Toby Forward

Magic Take Off

Illustrated by Ken Brown

PUFFIN BOOKS

For Ivan and Joyce

PUFFIN BOOKS

Published by the Penguin Group
Penguin Books Ltd, 27 Wrights Lane, London W8 5TZ, England
Penguin Books USA Inc., 375 Hudson Street, New York, New York 10014, USA
Penguin Books Australia Ltd, Ringwood, Victoria, Australia
Penguin Books Canada Ltd, 10 Alcorn Avenue, Toronto, Ontario, Canada M4V 3B2
Penguin Books (NZ) Ltd, 182–190 Wairau Road, Auckland 10, New Zealand

Penguin Books Ltd, Registered Offices: Harmondsworth, Middlesex, England

First published by Andersen Press Limited 1995
Published in Puffin Books 1997
1 3 5 7 9 10 8 6 4 2

Text copyright © Toby Forward, 1995
Illustrations copyright © Ken Brown, 1995
All rights reserved

The moral right of the author has been asserted

Made and printed in England by Clays Ltd, St Ives plc

'So far as I can make out, this is a recipe for Loss of Weight.'

H.G. Wells, *The Truth about Pyecraft*

Chapter 1

Bertie George pedalled along, whistling. His chin wobbled as his old black bike bumped on the cobbled street, but he was happy. Bertie was the best whistler in his school. He could do bird calls, huge shrieking salutes, tunes – he only needed to hear a tune once and he could do it perfectly, and he could even do the sound of a telephone bleeping. It was so good that you couldn't tell the difference. Once, when Bertie was in trouble for fighting at school, Mr Formalyn, the Headmaster, was trying to tell him off but the phone kept on interrupting. But every time that Mr Formalyn picked it up there was no one there.

'So, Bertie,' said Mr Formalyn, wagging a knobbly finger at him, 'let me tell you, my lad, that . . .'

Brrr. Brrrr. Brrr. Brrrr.

Mr Formalyn frowned. This was the third time.

'Yes, hello,' he said, snatching the phone.

Nothing.

He slammed it down.

'Now. Where was I?'

'Let me tell you, my lad,' said Bertie, helpfully.

'Yes. Well . . .'

Brrr. Brrrr.

Mr Formalyn leaped forward and grabbed it quickly.

'Yes!'

Nothing.

'This is the last time!' he yelled into the silent phone. 'The very last time.'

Slam.

'And if I ever catch you in a fight again, Bertie George, I'll . . .'

Brrr. Brrrr. . .

The phone was in Mr Formalyn's hand before Bertie saw him move.

'Now you listen to me!' shouted the Headmaster. 'If you've got nothing better to do than waste my time with stupid phone calls you should be locked up. You fool. Don't you know I'm a busy man?'

There was a small cough from the other end.

'Mr Formalyn?'

'Yes! Of course it is.' Mr Formalyn's moustache jumped up and down when he shouted. 'What are you playing about at?'

'I'm really very sorry to interrupt you . . .'

'Vicar?' said Mr Formalyn, recognising the voice.

'Er, yes. Is it an inconvenient time?'

Mr Formalyn blushed. 'Oh, er no. I'm . . . That is, I'm so sorry I . . . I don't suppose you called before?'

'No, this is my first try,' said the Vicar.

'Well, you see,' said Mr Formalyn, and he gave a little laugh, to try to apologise. 'That is, my phone . . .' He waved Bertie away and pointed to the door.

Bertie closed the door behind him. Waited. Heard the Headmaster carry on apologising. Then he blew gently between his teeth, curling up his tongue.

Brrr. Brrrr.

Mr Formalyn jumped, looked closely at the phone, frowned and went on apologising.

And he forgot all about Bertie and his fight. For that time.

But there were other fights. Lots of them. And Bertie started them all. And Bertie lost them all. But he kept on starting them.

Because Bertie was fat. Very fat. Bertie was the fattest boy they had ever seen at his school.

So, of course, nobody liked him really.

And they called him names. They called him Fatty, of course. And Piggy. And Wobbles. And Fatman. And Pigface. And Porker. Bertie hated all the names. But he especially hated Porker. His gran (Bertie lived with his gran) told him to ignore the names. And he was quite good at that. But he hated Porker so much that he couldn't ignore it. So he got into fights.

Sometimes, when he walked past people in the playground, someone grunted at him. Or oinked.

So Bertie was glad it was today. Because today was the first day of the holiday and there was a whole week without school. A whole week without anyone to call him names. A whole week without a fight. He was so happy that he nearly didn't bother to eat a chocolate egg with a creamy filling as he rode along. Nearly.

Mmmm. He licked a sticky lip, turned a sharp corner and plunged down a narrow lane. Bertie gripped the handlebars of the old black bike and wobbled happily along the cobbles to Pie Craft, the oldest and smallest and best pie shop in the whole world.

'Hey! Here's Pigface!'

'Oink!'

'Oink!'

'Grunt!'

'Porker!'

Bertie pointed his bike at a group of children from his school, pounded his feet down on the pedals and charged at them.

Chapter 2

It was wonderful.

The children leaped away screaming.

One knocked over a huge pile of oranges in front of the greengrocer's, and Mr Kelp jumped out and fetched him an enormous clip round the ear.

Another ran into the butcher's and got tangled up in a string of sausages.

The next one was Norman, Bertie's greatest enemy. He jumped into the air and landed right in the huge wicker basket on the front of Bertie's bike. His mouth dropped open and he gaped at Bertie in terror as Bertie pushed the pedals down harder and harder making the bike rattle fiercely over the cobbles. Then he jammed on the brakes, did a skid swerve-and-stop and Norman fell out of the basket and straight into a horse trough full of slimy water.

Bertie propped the bike against the wall outside Pie Craft.

'Oink to you, too,' he said. And he went in.

Norman squelched out and dripped away along the lane.

'Morning, Mr Platten,' said Bertie brightly. He slapped his hands together, brushed some imaginary

12

dust of battle from his shirt and leaned against the dark wooden counter.

Mr Platten smiled. There was no imaginary dust on him. He was all over flour. Flour had turned his brown hair white. Flour smudged his pink cheeks. Flour dusted his pudgy nose. Flour lined his chin. His white jacket, his striped trousers, his shoes, his hands, his ears were all coated with a fine layer of flour. Mr Platten baked pies.

And such pies.

Bertie sniffed gently and a smile covered his round face.

'What is it today?' he asked.

'Oh,' said Mr Platten, 'you know. Steak and kidney, chicken and herb, rabbit and prune, aubergine and basil – with just a hint of spiced tomato, cheese and chives – with a garnish of rosemary glaze to make the pastry shine.' He looked at Bertie and grinned. For all his baking and his beautiful pies, Mr Platten was a tall, thin man, with small, gold spectacles which twinkled when he looked at you. Bertie had never been able to work out how it was that all the rest of Mr Platten was covered in flour, but his spectacles were always as bright and clear as a lark's song.

'I know that,' said Bertie.

Mr Platten's eyebrows shot up in mock surprise. 'Then goodness me, why do you ask?' he said.

Brrr. Brrrr.

Mr Platten turned to pick up the phone, but remembered just in time. He had been tricked this way before and learned his lesson.

'Wurrrr. Wurrrr. I don't think so,' he laughed.

'What's the special today?' asked Bertie.

Mr Platten left the shop. There was a clanging of heavy metal doors, then a blast of heat, then a delicious, delicate aroma of spices and herbs. Mr Platten reappeared, bearing before him a tray of the strangest pies Bertie had ever seen.

They were not round, nor square, nor oblong. They had no scalloped edges, nor pastry leaves. They were little triangular parcels, in thin pastry with wavy edges.

Bertie leaned forward.

'Mind your nose,' warned Mr Platten. 'Wurrrr.'

'What?' asked Bertie.

Mr Platten picked up a pie and tossed it from hand to hand, like a juggler. He laughed at himself. 'Wurrrr. Wurrrr. It's hot,' he said.

Bertie sighed.

Mr Platten managed to break a piece from the pie. It steamed in the clear morning sunshine. 'Try it,' he offered. 'But be careful.'

Bertie bit into it hesitantly.

'Mmmm.'

'Like it?' Mr Platten bit his.

Bertie nodded, a crumb of pastry clinging to his lips.

'Wonderful.'

'Wurrrr. Wurrrr. Good.'

'What is it?'

'Samosa.'

'What?'

'Lentils, tomatoes, chick peas, onion, some special spice, all wrapped in the thinnest pastry.'

'It's the best pie I've ever tasted,' said Bertie.

'Good,' said Mr Platten. 'If they sell well I'll make them every day, not just as a special.'

'They'll sell,' promised Bertie.

'We'll soon find out,' said Mr Platten. 'Bring me your basket.'

Bertie went to his bike and unhooked the wicker basket. He laid it on the counter and started to pack it with bulging greaseproof paper bags. Mr Platten filled another bag with samosas and laid it carefully on the top.

'Here's your list,' he said to Bertie. 'The bags are all labelled, and I've put a map in as well.'

'I don't need a map,' said Bertie. 'I know where to go. They're all regulars.'

'Not this one,' said Mr Platten. He patted the top bag. 'This is a new order. For a Mr Gupta. He lives the other side of town.'

Bertie looked at the map. It seemed clear enough.

16

'If he likes the samosas we'll sell a lot more pies over there,' said Mr Platten.

'I'll go to him first,' said Bertie. 'While they're still warm.'

'Good boy,' said Mr Platten. 'And here. Here's yours. And your gran's.'

He handed Bertie two more bags.

'It's aubergine for your gran,' he said. 'And a few samosas for you. If that's all right? Wurrrr. Wurrrr.'

Bertie grinned. 'Thanks,' he said.

'Just the two,' said Mr Platten. 'But they're quite small. Would you like me to pop another one in?'

Bertie thought of the thin pastry and the delicious filling, and his mouth watered. 'No thanks,' he said. 'Two's fine.'

Mr Platten nodded.

He looked sadly through the diamond panes of the shop window as Bertie pedalled off, wobbling on the cobbles. And he shook his head sadly at how sad Bertie was because he was so fat, and wondered if he would ever be slim.

Because, and this was the strange thing, Bertie hardly ate anything at all at mealtimes, except for once a week when he ate a pie. All the children laughed when he got the job delivering pies for Pie Craft. 'You'll eat them all,' they jeered. 'That's how you get so fat, Porky!' And so Bertie had another fight, and he lost again.

17

But really, Bertie didn't eat the pies. He had one a week, as a treat. But most of the time he picked at his food.

'You'll never grow up strong if you don't eat,' said

his gran. And she put plates of liver and mashed potatoes, chicken and rice, grilled fish and steamed vegetables on the table, but he only picked at them, moved them around on the plate and then left them.

'I don't want it,' he said. 'I'm too fat.' And it was true. He was too fat.

'You'll grow out of it,' she promised.

Bertie laughed. 'That's the last thing I want,' he would say. 'To grow.'

'You'll lose weight,' she said.

But Bertie would leave all his food, go to his room and feel sad. Then, to make himself feel better, he would take out a bar of chocolate and eat it. And it worked. He did feel better. So he had another. And he felt better still. No matter how bad he felt, chocolate always made him feel better.

Then, at tea time, his gran would give him a boiled egg, and he would cut its head off, cut the toast into fingers, and then he would push it away. 'I'm not hungry. I'll get fat.'

'You'll lose weight, one day,' she promised. 'Eat your tea.'

'I'll never lose weight,' he groaned.

'You will,' she promised. 'One day.'

Bertie thought of the samosas as he pedalled along to Mr Gupta's. He stopped once to look at the map, and he put his hand on the paper bag to

19

feel the warmth of the pies.

He was a little confused by the strange streets, but he was determined not to go back to Mr Platten and say he couldn't find his way.

At last, after many twists and turns and after many wrong tries up dead ends, Bertie found the right street. He looked around. It was only a small street, off the main road, and there were no people around. He had never been in this part of the town before. At first, when he pedalled along the unfamiliar route he felt excited. It was an adventure. But now, away from everything he knew and recognised, he was a little nervous. He was sure he saw the corner of a curtain twitch and a hidden face peer out at him. But when he looked it was all still.

He checked the number of Mr Gupta's. 23. Counting the houses, he made his way along the street. It was a puzzle, so he took out a chocolate bar, with bubbles in it, just a light one really, to help him think. He munched it pensively.

But he needn't have bothered. Between 21 and 25 was a small shop, with nothing at all in the window, but a sign outside that said

GUPTA'S REMEDIES

Bertie leaned the bike against the wall, took the bag of samosas from the basket, pushed the door and went in.

A bell jangled above his head and Bertie jumped. He looked around, but he could not see anyone in the dim shop.

'Yes. Come in,' said a foreign voice.

Chapter 3

Bertie nearly turned and ran out of the shop.

'Come in, fat boy, come on in.'

Bertie felt himself go red and he would have clenched his hands if he had not been holding the paper bag with the pies in it.

He bounced in and slammed the door behind him. The bell jangled again, louder than before.

The shop was very dark. Bertie paused. Rows and rows of dusty jars stood along shelves behind the high counter. Their labels were faded and faintly-worded. Bulbous stoppers held their contents in secretive brown glass. A whole wall of drawers, with small brass handles and little tickets in brass holders, held more, dry ingredients.

The glass cases in front of the counter were clouded with neglect, and Bertie could hardly see through them to examine the instruments and machines, pots and bottles, boxes and tubes that huddled together.

'Come on in,' said the voice again.

Bertie couldn't see who was speaking. He looked around. But there was no one. He squinted, to make the most of the light. But there was no one. He looked up, as though the man might be floating in the air. Stupid Bertie, he could have kicked himself. Then he jumped back and felt for the handle of the door. A crocodile flew above him. At least seven feet long, with sharp claws flexed ready, and mouth slightly open in a hungry grin that displayed cruel teeth. And all around the crocodile, bats spread their leather wings and hovered.

Bertie yelped.

'All stuffed, fat boy. All stuffed,' the voice comforted him. And at last Bertie saw the man. He stepped out from behind a pile of whitish jars on the counter. 'Dead these long years,' he said. 'They hang from wires.'

Bertie relaxed his grip on the parcel, hoping he hadn't squashed the samosas.

'Not quite right for the crocodile,' the man said. 'Flying – not right at all, really. But there's no room for it anywhere else, and I can't let it go. Sentimental reasons. It belonged to my mother. It reminds me of her.'

He was no taller than Bertie. At least, he wouldn't have been if he'd taken his hat off. It was a wonderful hat, the shape of a pie – red, with gold embroidery and a small tassel that hung over the man's left ear. For the rest, he was dressed like a bank manager or a newsreader. Not at all foreign. 'But the bats are good,' he said. He flapped a brown hand above Bertie's head and the bats swayed realistically on their wires. 'See,' he smiled. 'Very good.'

Bertie held out his paper bag.

'Pies,' he said.

Mr Gupta looked inside. 'Samosas,' he said. He took one out, bit into it and sighed. He chewed softly, smiling. When it was all gone he spoke. 'Wonderful. I have not had such good samosas since I lost my poor mother.'

Bertie looked up at the crocodile. Perhaps the crocodile had eaten her?

'Oh, no!' said Mr Gupta, guessing Bertie's thoughts. 'She left that behind when she went. She's gone to Cheltenham. She writes every week, but you can't really send samosas through the post, can you?'

'I suppose not,' agreed Bertie.

'Like one?' Mr Gupta offered.

Bertie shook his head. 'I've got some in the basket. For later.'

Mr Gupta looked at him closely. 'Do you eat a lot of pies?'

'No.'

'You're very fat. For a boy who doesn't eat much.'

'I'll hit you if you say that again,' Bertie threatened him.

'Oh dear. Why do you say that?'

'You don't like me because I'm fat,' said Bertie.

'I do like you.'

'No one likes me because I'm fat.'

'And so you hit them?'

'Yes.'

Mr Gupta shook his head.

'What's the matter?' asked Bertie.

Mr Gupta put his face very close to Bertie's. 'I don't think they mind you being fat,' he said. 'If you gave them a chance, they might like you. But I think you don't like yourself.'

Bertie felt confused by this, but he quite liked Mr Gupta now, and decided he probably wasn't being rude, just foreign, so he forgot about hitting him.

'What do you sell?' he asked.

'Remedies.'

'What's a remedy?'

'Something that makes you better.'

'Medicine?'

'Sort of. Like medicine.'

Bertie examined the big pile of whitish jars. 'What are these?'

'Wart cream.'

'It gets rid of warts?'

'That's right.'

Bertie looked doubtful. 'There's a lot of it,' he said.

'Yes.'

'Are there lots of people with warts round here?'

'No. Of course not.'

'That's why you've got lots of jars left,' said Bertie. 'What's this?' He pointed to a bottle in the glass case.

'Cheek ointment,' said Mr Gupta.

'You rub it on your cheeks?' said Bertie. 'What for?'

'No,' said Mr Gupta. 'You drink it. It stops you being cheeky. Would you like some?'

Bertie stared at him.

'This one,' said Mr Gupta, stepping behind the counter and taking down a huge jar, 'is memory medicine. It helps you to remember everything. Very good before exams. You can't fail.'

'Wow,' said Bertie.

'But the trouble is,' said Mr Gupta, 'it's very dangerous, and if you take the wrong dose, just too little, or just too much, you come out in purple blotches and you stink. Flies buzz round you for a week. But it's very good, otherwise,' he said. 'Very good. Memory medicine.' He took the stopper out and sniffed it.

'How much do you have to take?' asked Bertie.

Mr Gupta frowned, turned the bottle round and round looking for a label, but there wasn't one. 'I can't remember,' he admitted.

Bertie took a small pot, like a pepper pot, with a hole in the top. He held it out to Mr Gupta with

27

a puzzled look on his face.

'Ah,' said Mr Gupta. 'That's not for sale. That's elephant powder. I use that every day.'

'Made out of elephants?'

'Oh, dear me, no. Elephants are far too rare to make them into powder. Whatever gave you that idea? Still, it's time I used it.'

'What's it for?'

Mr Gupta opened the front door, making the bell jangle again. He sprinkled a little of the powder on the step and closed the door again. 'Just a little every day,' he said. 'And it keeps the elephants away.'

Bertie laughed at him. 'You're mad,' he said. 'There aren't any elephants for thousands of miles from here.'

Mr Gupta put the shaker beneath the counter. 'Good, isn't it?' he said. 'See how it works?'

Bertie stopped laughing.

'Now,' said Mr Gupta. 'If there's nothing else, I won't keep you from your work, fat boy. Please tell Mr Platten the samosas were delicious. I'll be back for more another day. Goodbye.' And he gave Bertie a strange look.

Bertie hesitated. He hated being called fat boy again, just as he was getting to like Mr Gupta. Then, he had an idea. He remembered his gran's voice. 'You'll lose weight one day, Bertie.'

28

He looked around at all the bottles and jars and drawers.

'Mr Gupta?'

'Yes?'

'Have you got anything to make me lose weight?'

Mr Gupta half smiled. Then he thought. 'Well,' he said, 'I might.'

'Can I have some? How much?'

Mr Gupta tapped his lips with his finger. 'I didn't say I had. I said I might.'

'Please,' said Bertie. 'Please.'

Chapter 4

Mr Gupta took a bunch of keys from his pocket. He selected a small silver one and turned it in the lock of a little cupboard that Bertie had not noticed before. He took a tiny bottle from the cupboard, locked the door again, and turned to Bertie.

'I don't know,' he said. 'It's very powerful stuff.'

Bertie imagined himself after he had taken the medicine. After he had lost weight. He would be happy. People would stop calling him names. He would make friends. 'Please,' he said, 'I must have it. I'll pay you anything.'

Mr Gupta looked at him very hard. 'You're sure you want to lose weight?'

'Yes.'

'Will it make any difference?' he asked.

'Of course. People will like me.'

Mr Gupta thought again. Bertie felt that he would burst if he didn't get that bottle. He wanted to grab it out of Mr Gupta's hand and run out of the shop.

'All right,' said Mr Gupta. 'But you must take the right dose, or it will be very dangerous.'

'How much?' croaked Bertie.

'One teaspoonful every night for a week,' said

Mr Gupta. 'No more. No less.'

Bertie agreed. 'How much does it cost?'

'You brought me these samosas,' said Mr Gupta. 'So it is free to you.'

Bertie thanked him and ran out of the shop, banging the door and jangling the bell.

He sped round the town delivering his pies. He pedalled so furiously that his cheeks wobbled and his tummy bounced above the crossbar. He ate seven bars of chocolate, just to keep his energy going and to take his mind off how wonderful it would be when he lost weight.

Mr Platten's eyes sparkled at him when he reported in at Pie Craft to say it was all done.

'Did you find Mr Gupta?' he asked.

'Oh, yes,' said Bertie. 'And he really liked the samosas, and he said he'll buy lots more.'

'Good,' said Mr Platten, and a little cloud of flour rose up from him in pleasure. 'Goodbye then, Bertie.'

''Bye,' shouted Bertie as he bounced away over the cobbles.

Gran ate her pie and looked at Bertie.

'Don't you like those new pies?'

'Mmm?'

'I said, don't you like those new pies? You can have mine if you like.'

Bertie looked at his plate. He had pulled the samosas to pieces and pushed them around his plate, but he had not eaten any of them.

'No, they're fine,' he said. 'But I'm not hungry.' He pretended to yawn. 'I'll go to bed.'

Gran looked at him kindly. 'You'll lose weight one day,' she said.

'Yes,' said Bertie. 'I will. I know.'

'That's good,' said Gran.

Bertie sat on his bed and looked at the tiny bottle. He remembered the purple blotches and the stink for the memory medicine, and he thought that Mr Gupta had not told him what would happen if he took the wrong dose of this one. But perhaps it didn't matter. Perhaps Mr Gupta was wrong all the time and any dose was dangerous?

He munched his way through a thoughtful bar of chocolate.

One teaspoonful.

He took the stopper out. He sniffed. No smell. He munched another bar of chocolate.

He poured a little on to a spoon. No colour.

He munched another bar of chocolate and poured the medicine back into the bottle.

To be honest, he was scared. Mr Gupta was a funny sort of person. And the shop was very odd, with the bats and crocodile. Still, you couldn't just go round giving people poison. They'd lock you up.

So it must be all right.

He took the bottle again. One teaspoon every night for a week. That was seven teaspoons. No point in waiting a week. He measured out seven teaspoons into a glass, and one extra 'for the pot', the way Gran did when she made tea. He lifted the glass, closed his eyes, held his nose and . . . swallowed the lot.

Then he went to sleep.

Bertie woke up when his gran came in to say goodnight. She kissed him lightly and he felt his stomach. Fat.

He moved and turned when an owl hooted outside his window, and he pinched his leg, just to feel it. Fat.

The milkman rattled a bottle lightly on the step at half past four. Bertie stirred. His head was funny, and he felt a little giddy. He prodded a cautious finger into his side. Fat.

When at last the sunlight threw a splash of light over Bertie's eyes and he knew it was morning he squeezed his eyes together tight, too frightened to dare to hope that he had lost weight. He felt his tummy, his bottom, his legs, his cheeks. Fat. All fat. As fat as ever. He groaned, turned over, bumped his head on something hard, opened his eyes and screamed with terror.

Chapter 5

Gran rushed in.

'What's the matter?'

The bed was empty.

'Bertie?'

She looked around. Nothing.

'Oh,' groaned Bertie.

His gran looked under the bed.

'Where are you? What's the matter?'

'Here,' said Bertie.

'Don't play games,' she said, beginning to sound cross.

'Up here,' said Bertie.

Gran looked up and saw Bertie up in the corner of the bedroom, over the door.

'Get down at once,' she said. 'You'll hurt yourself.'

'I can't,' said Bertie. 'I'm stuck.'

Gran looked at him. She was puzzled as well as cross. Both Bertie's hands were waving at her. He didn't seem to be holding on to anything.

'How are you doing it?' she asked.

'I'm not,' he said. 'Look.'

And he waved his hands even more violently, and his legs. And he drifted across the ceiling.

Gran jumped faster than Bertie had ever thought she could. She swung the window shut with a bang.

'I don't know how you're doing it,' she said, 'but stop. You could have fallen out of that window.'

'I don't think so,' said Bertie sadly. 'I'm floating.'

'What?'

'I mean,' he explained, 'I wouldn't fall at all. I'd just float off.'

Gran jumped up and managed to get a hand to Bertie's leg. She pulled. He drifted down towards her like a balloon.

Bertie smiled gratefully.

'You don't weigh anything,' said Gran.

'No.'

'Well.' Whenever Gran said 'well' like that she pulled a face and folded her arms. So she did that now and let go of Bertie.

As soon as she had let go of Bertie he floated back up to the ceiling and bumped his head.

'Ow.'

'Sorry.'

Bertie gave her a reproachful look and rubbed his head.

Gran reached up and pulled him back down.

It was like hauling in a huge kite. At times she felt that he was going to lift her off the floor with him.

Panting at the effort, she managed to hold him

almost down to her own level. But as soon as she loosened her grip on him he started to lift off again.

'Under the bed,' she said.

'What?'

'Climb under the bed.'

Bertie grabbed hold of the edge of the bed and dragged himself along until he could climb beneath it.

'It's a bit dusty,' he complained.

'You can't clean everywhere,' said Gran.

Bertie sneezed.

Gran let go.

Bertie was still floating just above the floor, but the bed stopped him going up to the ceiling.

'What have you done?' she asked.

Bertie explained about the medicine.

'To make you thin?' she asked.

'Yes.'

'Well it hasn't worked, has it? You're as fat as ever.'

Bertie nodded.

'Are you sure?' said Gran.

'Yes. I asked him for something to make me lose weight.'

Gran frowned. 'That's not the same thing,' she said.

'It's what you always said. "You'll lose weight, one day." '

'I know,' said Gran. 'But it's just a way of talking. What you've done is lose all your weight, but not your fat.'

Bertie groaned.

'Oh, why did you do it?' she asked him, with a sharp tone to her voice.

'So that people would like me. When I'm thin.'

'They'd like you a good deal more if you stopped trying to hit them,' said Gran.

'I wouldn't hit them if I was thin,' said Bertie.

'You'd find a reason,' said Gran. 'Now, we'll have to put the weight back on.'

'How?'

'Wait here,' she said.

Bertie didn't like it under the bed. It wasn't just the dust. There were old chocolate wrappings that he had hidden there, but no chocolate. And there were bits of stuff that looked like toe nails. And there was something on his leg that he was sure was a spider but he was too fat to turn round in the narrow space to find out.

He sneezed again.

Gran's ankles appeared.

Then her face, as she bent down.

'Breakfast,' she said.

'What is it?'

'Porridge.'

'I hate porridge,' said Bertie.

'You've never tried it. Porridge is heavy,' said Gran. 'You eat lots of porridge, you'll get heavy again.'

So Bertie ate the porridge. And it wasn't as bad as he thought it would be. And toast. He ate four slices of toast. And that wasn't too bad either.

'That should do it,' said Gran. 'Come on out.

Bertie slid out from under the bed. As soon as he was clear he rose slowly up to the ceiling and bumped his head.

'Ow.'

Gran bit her lip.

'More porridge?'

Bertie shook his head.

'It was all right,' he said. 'But I'm full.'

'You should be heavy,' said Gran.

'I feel heavy.'

Gran picked up the bottle and looked at it.

'Where did you get this?'

Bertie explained.

Gran went and got her best hat out. It was one with a small bunch of grapes on the brim and a tiny bird made out of blue and yellow feathers.

'I'll go and get him to give you something to make you heavy again,' she said.

Bertie bounced against the ceiling. 'Please,' he said. 'Oh, please go.'

He explained as well as he could where Mr

Gupta's shop was. Gran looked for the map that Mr Platten had drawn, but there was no sign of it anywhere. She shook her head when Bertie told her the name of the street. 'I've lived here all my life,' she said, 'but I've never heard of it.' And she made sure the window was shut tightly and left Bertie floating in the air.

Bertie hauled himself across the room and peeped out of the window. He just managed to see the bunch of grapes and the little blue and yellow bird over the top of the hedge. And then Gran was gone.

Right. What now?

Chapter 6

It's funny how you don't notice how easy things are until they're hard, Bertie grumbled to himself. Take getting dressed. When you can stand on the floor to get dressed it's easy. You take your pyjamas off, drop them, then pick up your trousers and things and put them on. Easy. But, when you're trying to hold on to the bed at the same time to stop yourself drifting up to the ceiling, it's not so simple.

So, Bertie took a long time getting dressed, and he bumped his head a lot of times. It was maddening to put his leg in his trousers and find himself turning upside down and landing on the ceiling.

At last, he was done.

He opened the bedroom door, very carefully, and pulled himself downstairs, gripping the banister. He tied himself to the rail with the cord of his dressing-gown, like a mountain climber. It was hard work, but he felt a lot safer.

It was a bit of a problem getting into the kitchen. At first he tried standing upside down on the ceiling and walking, but he was so light he couldn't put his weight down, or up, on the ceiling. He just bobbed about like a rubber dinghy on a pond. So he crawled. It seemed that the more of him there was up on the ceiling the easier it was to move.

Not that it was ever easy.

He was glad when Gran came home.

'Have you got it?' he asked.

Gran put a big paper bag on the kitchen table.

'I couldn't find the shop,' she said.

Bertie banged his shin against the top of the kitchen door.

'Ow. But it's the only shop in the street.'

'I couldn't even find the street,' she said.

Bertie jumped up and down (or, rather, down and up) in frustration. 'I told you all about it.'

'So did Mr Platten,' said Gran. She brushed a smudge of flour from her sleeve. 'I went to the pie shop.'

Bertie went as white as the flour.

'You didn't tell him? You didn't tell Mr Platten?' he shouted.

'Calm down,' said Gran. ''Course I didn't. Think I'm a fool?'

Bertie didn't answer.

'I just said I wanted to go there for some medicine,' she said. 'But he said he'd never heard of Mr Gupta.'

Gran looked at Bertie very hard when she said this.

Bertie's jaw fell open. Well, it didn't exactly fall

because he was up on the ceiling and it went up not down. It was funny, how everything was different now he was on the ceiling. Gran, for instance, was so small from up there.

'Time to eat,' she said.

The pies were delicious. Gran made mashed potatoes, and she sliced onions very thin and made a special gravy with them to pour over the pies. Bertie ate two whole pies, mashed potatoes and some green beans. 'These are all right,' he said. He had never eaten beans before.

Gran nodded.

Bertie had tied himself to the chair with his dressing-gown cord and was more or less safe. He was still so light that the chair hovered about three inches above the floor, but he did not drift up to the ceiling. The only trouble was he couldn't make any sudden movements. If he knocked his hand against the edge of the table he drifted away across the kitchen, like a hovercraft.

Gran put a dish of apple and blackberry crumble in front of him. She poured creamy smooth custard over it.

'I hate . . .' began Bertie.

'Eat it up,' said Gran. And she gave his chair a little nudge with her foot so that Bertie drifted over towards the fridge. Just to remind him. 'See?'

'All right.'

Gran steered him back to the table, with a small smile.

'It's like pushing the trolley in the supermarket,' she said. 'Only lighter.'

Bertie took the spoon and frowned. He ate the first mouthful hesitantly. Then took another, more willingly. Then another. The rest went down very quickly.

Bertie was surprised how hungry he was.

'I wouldn't mind a bar of chocolate, when I've finished,' he said.

'Chocolate's no good,' said Gran. 'Not heavy enough. Have some more pudding.'

Bertie really was full after the second helping, and he didn't want any chocolate.

'How's the chair?' he asked.

Gran bent down and looked. She could still put her hand between the legs of the chair and the floor.

'About the same.'

Bertie sighed. 'It's hopeless.'

Gran patted him on the shoulder to encourage him and the chair bobbed up and down like a raft. 'It'll be all right,' she said.

Bertie stuck out a foot and the chair went floating away.

Gran cleared the table, humming a little tune.

'All that porridge and pies and pudding,' said Bertie. 'And I'm still the same. I don't weigh anything.'

Gran washed the plates.

'I'll never go out of the house again,' said Bertie. 'I'm locked in.'

'Oh, I don't think so,' said Gran.

'Think of it,' said Bertie. 'I'd float away. You'd never see me again.'

Gran wiped the dishes, put the cloth over the front of the oven to dry. 'Not if we make you heavy,' she said.

'We've tried,' said Bertie. 'It doesn't work.'

'Well, it's early days yet,' said Gran. 'A few more pies and things and who knows? But, I didn't mean that.'

'What, then?' said Bertie.

'Come up to your bedroom,' said Gran.

Bertie rather liked the way he could drift up the stairs while Gran puffed her way behind him.

He tied himself to the end of the bed and hung halfway between floor and ceiling.

'Now,' said Gran. 'Look at this.'

Bertie could have cried when he saw her take out his bag of marbles.

'That's no good,' he said.

'Put them in your pockets.'

He did. He drifted down a couple of inches.

'Now,' said Gran, looking round. 'What else?'

Bertie became excited. 'My money box,' he said.

47

'Over there.'

It took Gran a long time to go back to the kitchen for a blunt knife and come back up the stairs, and then rest a minute to get her breath back, and then slide the coins out of the pig.

'You've got a lot here,' she said.

'It's what Mr Platten pays me,' said Bertie. 'It's my chocolate money.'

'Here we are.'

But Bertie's pockets were full. So he took out the marbles (drifting up in the air a little higher) then put the coins in his pockets, then he got Gran to put the marbles back into the bag and tie it to his ankle. He came lower still, and was almost standing upright, with the weight of the marbles pulling his leg down. Gran tied a string of conkers round his other ankle, and both legs began to drift down together. Bertie was now hovering in the air, quite upright, about three feet from the floor.

'Great!' he cried. 'You've done it!'

He jumped forward to give Gran a hug, whizzed past her and through the bedroom door.

'Help!'

Gran ran after him and found him rebounding off the bathroom door and straight into her arms.

Bertie clutched her and came to an unsteady halt.

Gran found herself lifted slightly from the floor as she held on to him.

'Not quite right yet,' she said.

'No,' agreed Bertie. And he bit his lip.

'I know,' said Gran. 'Take your shirt off.'

While Bertie took off his shirt Gran went back down to the kitchen again.

'We'll move to a bungalow if this goes on,' she complained when she had got her breath back again.

But Bertie was more interested in the apron and the little piles of metal weights she had brought.

He put on the apron and Gran dropped the weights into the deep pocket at the front.

'I don't know how I'll be able to cook without my scales,' she grumbled.

'Wonderful,' said Bertie. He put his shirt on over the apron and stood, firmly, if rather anxiously, on the floor again.

'Right!' he said. 'That's it. I'm off.'

'Off?' said Gran. 'You can't.'

'You just watch me,' said Bertie. 'I'm going to find Mr Gupta.'

'No!' said Gran. 'You'll float away.'

Bertie opened a cupboard and took out a bar of chocolate with lots of raisins and bits of crunchy things in it. 'Just to keep me going,' he said. Then he looked at it, remembered the pies and the crumble and felt very full. 'I'll have it when I get back,' he said, and put it away.

'Now, Bertie,' said Gran. 'Wait another day. You'll be heavier tomorrow – after more porridge.'

Bertie walked away, purposefully, which was difficult, because he sort of bounced up and down when he walked, like a man on the moon. And he jingled and clanked, from the coins and the marbles.

'No,' he said. 'I'm going.'

'Oh,' said Gran. And she watched him wheel the old black bike down the path.

Chapter 7

Bertie made quite sure he was safe. He tied himself to the bike with the dressing-gown cord.

It was so easy. The bike whizzed along. Bertie bounced and wobbled along on the saddle, but he was so light he hardly had to push the pedals at all.

He turned down the narrow lane, flew past Pie Craft, with a wave to Mr Platten, and out of sight. The cobbles made the bike judder and jangle, but Bertie wasn't shaken up at all. Except.

Except.

Because he was so light, Bertie didn't feel himself shaking about on the bike as it skimmed across the bumpy cobbles. He felt good. He felt the fresh breeze in his face as he sped along. He felt the rattling of the handlebars. He felt his hair sweep back with the speed. He heard the clanking of the wheels. He saw the shops and houses fly past him. But, he was so light he did not feel himself shake on the saddle. He was not shaken up at all. Except.

Except.

Except the metal weights were shaken out of the pockets of his apron, down the legs of his trousers, and they fell – clank, clank, clank, on the cobbles.

And the string round the conkers was shaken loose and they slid off and fell from his ankle – clunk, clunk, clunk.

And the marbles jiggled and joggled and bounced their way out of the bag on his other ankle, and they fell on to the cobbles as well – ping, pang, pung.

So, except for all these things, Bertie wasn't shaken at all.

And as the marbles and the conkers and the metal weights fell on to the cobblestones, Bertie became lighter and lighter and lighter. And the faster he went, and the lighter he grew, the less Bertie felt the shaking of the bike and the happier he was.

'Wow!' he called. 'This is great. I'm flying over the cobbles. I'm so light. Look out, Mr Gupta! Here I come!'

And he pushed the pedals down harder and harder. And the bike went faster and faster. And the last marble, and the last conker, and the last metal weight dropped to the cobbles – plunk – clunk – clank.

So that, slowly, inch by inch, like a duck leaving the water, the bike lifted off the cobbles and up, up, into the air. And Bertie, tied to it by the cord of his dressing-gown was lifted as well.

Bertie's rise was so slow that at first he didn't notice.

The first thing he noticed was how quiet the tyres were.

The second thing he noticed was how smooth the ride was.

The third thing he noticed was how still the handlebars were.

The fourth thing he noticed was how easy it was to push the pedals.

The last thing he noticed was the upstairs bedroom window of a house.

Bertie rode past a window cleaner at the top of his ladder, polishing a pane with his leather.

'Afternoon,' said the man, with a cheerful nod.

'Lovely day,' said Bertie.

And, at the same time, they blinked, looked again, and jumped.

Now, it wasn't so bad for Bertie when he jumped, because he was tied to a bike and was floating in the air.

But, when the window cleaner jumped, he fell off his ladder, into a rose bush, and ended up with a bottom full of prickles and a bucket on his head.

Bertie's jump sent him spinning round in a new direction, and it jerked the bike higher still, up above the houses, round the chimney pots, over the tiles, up again, higher and higher, round again, till Bertie's head was spinning faster than the bike, and he didn't know where he was. He pushed his feet hard on the pedals, desperately trying to send the bike back to the cobbled lane. But all he did was make it go faster than ever, up and up, till the town was far below and behind him and he was flying away.

Now, Bertie didn't like heights very much. But this time he was more worried about floating right away, up and up and up until he burst a huge hole in the ozone layer, than falling back down to the ground.

He tried to control the bike.

If he pedalled there was some sort of feeling that he was moving forward.

He stopped pedalling to test this out.

He still kept moving forward.

Bertie stuck his finger in his mouth and sucked it. Then he held it up to test the wind. It wasn't the pedalling that was moving the bike, it was the wind. He turned the handlebars. The bike turned round, but now Bertie was going backwards.

He sighed.

He had no control over the bike at all. It just went wherever the wind sent him.

Bertie folded his arms and looked around him.

The ground was a very long way off, and it seemed to move as the wind pushed him along. But it wasn't getting any further away. He wasn't going any higher. So that was good.

But he was still worried. He needed to think. He

put his hand in his pocket for a chocolate bar.

Empty.

Nothing.

No chocolate.

He had left the bar in his bedroom because the pies had made him so full.

Bertie would have to work out an answer without chocolate.

Brrr. Brrrr.

Bertie picked up an imaginary phone.

'Yes?' he said.

'That's right.'

'Up in the air.'

'No, don't laugh,' said Bertie. 'It's true.'

He waited, listening.

'No. I don't know what to do. How am I ever going to get down?'

He waited again, hoping.

Chapter 8

Bertie tried breathing out all the air in his lungs, to make himself heavier. Air was light, wasn't it? But he didn't go down. He leaned forward and let the air out of the front tyre. But he still didn't go down.

He closed his eyes and thought of heavy things – stones, school puddings, tractors, the Taj Mahal. He thought and thought and thought and kept his eyes screwed up really tight.

Then.

All of a sudden.

He opened them.

Quickly.

But he was just as high up as he had ever been.

The sky was clear and the sun was gentle on his back. The fields below were green and gold and, best of all, a beautiful, ridged brown where they had been ploughed. Lanes scribbled their patterns in the landscape. Villages, with blue ponds, and ducks, and friendly swirls of houses grouped around a green, passed beneath him, but no one thought to look up. Bertie was having quite a good time, in a way. And if he could only be sure that he could get down safely he would have enjoyed himself. But even the tallest steeples were too far below for him to be able to reach down and grab one and pull himself back to earth.

What if a jet plane came his way and crashed into him?

Bertie shuddered.

While he was over one village a group of ducks splashed their way along the top of the water with webbed feet, flapping their wings, and then they were off. Clumsy when they ran, they were graceful in the air. They stretched out in a line and flew up and passed Bertie, very close.

'Help!' he called, remembering stories where animals came to people's rescue. 'Help! Come close and I'll grab you. You can tow me down.'

He felt very foolish when the ducks flew past without even looking at him.

'Help,' he said, quietly. 'Please.'

But they flew past and on and out of sight.

Bertie started to admit to himself that he was more than worried. He was frightened. Very frightened.

Then, in front of him, hovering in the air, was a huge face, with great staring eyes and a wide mouth gaping at him.

Bertie shrieked.

He gripped the handlebars and slammed on the

brakes. But, of course, there was nothing for the tyres to grip on to, so the wind pushed him forward and straight into the open mouth.

Flapping jaws folded round Bertie. A bony skeleton trapped him. He twisted round and round, trying to escape, but only became more and more tangled in a net of fear.

The wind tugged him. He pedalled faster than ever, but could not escape.

A strong pull jerked him down. And down. And down. And down. Until. BUMP. He hit the ground.

'Well,' said a kind voice. 'What's this?'

Bertie pushed aside a flap of loose plastic. He peered out of the mouth of a fierce face, and saw that he had been hauled down by an old woman with a large, monster kite.

'Quickly!' he said. 'Please. Tie me up.'

The woman laughed. And that made her cheeks wobble.

'Tie you up?' she said. 'I'd have thought you wanted me to cut you free.'

'No, you mustn't,' said Bertie. 'I'll float up again if you do. Please. I'll hit you if you don't,' he said, hesitantly.

The woman looked at him curiously. 'Well, you are a one,' she said. 'What would you do that for? Still, if it's what you want. I'll tie you up.'

She made one end of the twine fast to the handlebars of the bike and tied the other to the gate.

'Will that do?'

'Thanks,' said Bertie.

The woman pulled the kite away from him. It wasn't easy because he kept on bobbing up away from her. The struts were snapped and twisted, skeleton arms that had embraced Bertie. 'These are no use any more,' she said. But the main part of the kite was tough and she was able to pull it over Bertie's head. 'Just a few small rips,' she decided. 'We can soon fix them. Cup of tea?'

'What?'

'Would you like a cup of tea?'

'Yes, please,' said Bertie.

'How can we do this?' she asked.

'Careful,' warned Bertie.

'I know,' she said. She untied the twine from the gate, but made sure that she held on to it very tightly. 'All right?'

'So far.'

'Come on, then.' And she waddled up the garden path, pulling Bertie behind her like a kite. Her cottage was small and old, with a mossy slate roof and worn red bricks. With a sharp tug she brought Bertie right to the ground, ran backwards much faster than Bertie thought a fat old lady would be able to, jerking him after her. He knocked his head on the low wooden beam over the front door, but he was so pleased to be inside and safe again that he really didn't mind. Not much, anyway. Well, hardly at all.

'I'll shut the door,' she said. 'Just to be on the safe side.'

Bertie hung in the air, his head bumping against the low ceiling. The bicycle kept him upright.

'Are you all right?' she asked.

'My bottom hurts a bit,' he said.

'Your bottom? I thought it was your head you banged?'

'Yes, but I've been on this bike a long time, and I'm sore.'

'Can't you get off?'

Bertie untied the cord of his dressing-gown. The bike fell to the floor with a terrible clatter.

'Sorry.'

Bertie floated right up, so that he was lying on the ceiling. Without the conkers or the marbles, or the coins, or the metal weights, there was nothing to pull him down at all.

'I'm sorry I said I'd hit you,' said Bertie.

'China or Indian?' said the lady.

Bertie looked puzzled. 'Would you like China or Indian tea?' she explained.

'Milk, please,' said Bertie.

'Good.'

'But I don't think I can drink it up here,' he said.

'How do you do that?' asked the woman.

Bertie sighed.

'Doesn't matter,' she said. 'Am I to understand that you can't come down?'

'No.'

'No?'

'No.'

'No, I'm wrong, or no, you can't?'

'No, I can't.'

'All right. What shall I call you? I'm Molly.'

'Bertie.'

'That's nice.'

Bertie, who didn't specially like being called Bertie, was pleased that she said this, and he smiled at her.

'And that's a nice smile,' said Molly, who had one just as pleasant to give back to him. Which she did.

'I'll make the tea, while I'm thinking,' she said. And she bustled about in the little kitchen, clinking cups and tinkling spoons and filling a little blue teapot with steaming water and black, aromatic tea. 'Have you always been like this?' she asked as she worked.

'No,' said Bertie. 'It's new.'

'What happened?'

Bertie told her about the medicine and about the mix-up between losing weight and getting thin.

'Oh, dear,' she laughed. 'That is a problem.'

'Yes,' said Bertie.

'But did it matter all that much?'

'What?'

'Being fat? I'm fat, but I don't mind.'

'You're old,' said Bertie, before he could stop himself. 'Oh, I'm sorry. I didn't mean that.'

'Yes, you did,' said Molly. 'You didn't mean to say it, but you did mean it. Because I am old. Does that make such a lot of difference?'

Bertie told her about Norman and the names, and about not having any friends.

'People don't call you names when you're grown up,' he said.

Molly pursed her lips. 'Not in the same way,' she said, 'and not to your face. But perhaps if you didn't mind so much, then they wouldn't do it.'

'They do it because I'm fat,' said Bertie.

'No,' said Molly. 'They do it because you mind.'

Bertie didn't really understand the bit about it being different when you're grown up, but he was beginning to believe the other bit. The bit about people not liking him because he hit them rather than because he was fat. He frowned, trying to take it in. He was getting used to Molly, and to the new idea, so he started to look around her cottage.

It was very old, with walls that bulged out in odd places, and low, black beams, and a huge fireplace that took up the whole of one wall. And there were books. Books everywhere: on shelves, on tables, behind the chairs, on the piano, piled up on the floor. Everywhere. And strange pictures, with patterns and diagrams and maps of the stars at night, and drawings of herbs and wild flowers and mysterious temples with birds hovering round their towers, and all sorts of magical things.

She was a witch.

It wasn't tea she was making. It didn't smell like any tea Bertie had ever smelt before. It was perfumed and Molly didn't put any milk in it.

She was a witch.

Now, last week, Bertie would have wanted to rush out of the little cottage, pedal away as fast as he could and never look back in case she turned into a toad. But today, today the very thing he needed was a witch. She could give him a magical potion to make him heavy again.

He looked down at Molly. She was short, fat, wrinkled, with flat feet that made her waddle when she walked, and grey hair that was all long and straggly and tied back in a bun, not neat and curled and brushed the way an old lady's hair ought to be.

She was a witch.

Right.

This was it.

'Now, I think we can get you down,' she said, sipping from her elixir.

Chapter 9

Molly lifted the china cup to her lips and sipped.

Bertie held his breath.

What if she was going to turn herself into a frog, or a snake, or a bat?

Or what if she was going to make herself weightless as well, and float up to the ceiling to join him.

Witches were funny things. If they liked you they could help you, but if they took against you then you were in big trouble.

'Look,' said Bertie. 'I don't mind that you're a witch. I like witches. So, will you help me to get heavy again, please?'

Molly gave a little sigh of satisfaction, put the cup to one side and smiled at Bertie. 'Lovely,' she said.

Bertie waited for her to change.

'Now,' she said. 'I'm sorry to have my tea before you have your milk. Very bad manners of me. But I was so shaken up by finding you tangled up in my kite.' She pulled his leg. 'It's not every day I pull a bicyclist out of the sky, you know. So, I needed a nice cup of tea.'

Bertie agreed.

'Now,' said Molly. 'I'm sorry. What did you say?'

'Nothing,' said Bertie. He was very embarrassed about calling her a witch. He had an idea.

Brrr. Brrrr.

Brrr. Brrrr.

Molly put her head on one side and listened.

'That's very clever,' she said. 'How do you do it?'

Bertie blushed.

The noise stopped.

'Can you get me down?' he said. 'Please.'

Molly opened a cupboard and a pile of stuff tumbled out of it.

She rummaged around, throwing things over her shoulder.

Bertie watched a straw hat, very flat and very round, skim across the room. It was followed by what looked like a pair of yellow silk pyjamas with a red dragon on them. Then, a pair of shoes on blocks, a flat cap, a clay pipe, a stuffed pigeon, a pile of chopsticks, a warm scarf, a pair of tin trousers – 'Aha,' said Molly as they flew over her shoulder – a football boot – 'No,' – a whistle, a peaked cap with GWR on it, a paper tiger, a beer bottle, a rubber spider – 'Got it,' said Molly, and she appeared, holding a pair of lumpy shoes.

She picked up the tin trousers and handed them up to Bertie.

'Put these on,' she said.

'They're a bit tight.'

'Try them under your own trousers.'

Bertie blushed.

'Oh, all right,' said Molly, and she turned away. 'I dug those up,' she said, 'in China. That's where I got interested in kites. They're over a thousand years old.'

'The kites?' said Bertie.

Molly turned to answer him and saw Bertie struggling to pull the tin trousers over his underpants. 'Whoops. Sorry.' She turned away again. 'No, the trousers. They're ancient Chinese armour. Lots of metal discs sewn on to cotton breeches. How are they?'

'Fine,' said Bertie. 'You can look now.'

Bertie was floating six inches above the carpet, quite upright.

'Splendid,' said Molly. 'Here.' And she gave him the lumpy shoes.

'These are Dutch,' said Bertie. 'Clogs.'

'Clogs,' agreed Molly. 'But they're from round here. My granddad used to wear them to go to work in.'

Bertie's feet settled firmly on the floor. The clogs were made of wood, with leather tops, and iron nails shining all around the edge. 'They're good,' he said, surprised at how comfortable they were.

Molly handed him a glass of cold milk and a plate

of buttered fruit buns. Bertie scoffed the lot.

'I say,' said Molly. 'That's pretty good.'

'Sorry,' said Bertie. 'I was hungry. I mean, I'm trying to eat a lot of stuff to make me heavy again.'

'Good-oh,' said Molly. 'Have another.' So Bertie did. He had never liked buttered buns before.

'How did you know it was me?' he asked. 'It fools everyone.'

'What was you?'

'Brrr. Brrrr.'

Molly laughed. 'I haven't got a phone.'

Bertie wanted to change the subject. 'Do you come from China?'

'No, but I lived there a long time. I did history things, digging up old pots, flying kites. They have lots of strange medicine and potions over there.'

'You haven't got anything, have you? Something to make me heavy again?'

'Sorry. They don't work anyway, and they're mostly things like how to get revenge on an enemy, or how to make a girl fall in love with you.'

'Ugh,' said Bertie.

'Yes,' agreed Molly.

'I'd better be getting home,' said Bertie.

'I expect so,' she said.

Bertie picked up his bike. 'You haven't got a pump, have you? I let the air out of the tyre.'

'Sorry. And look, you bent the wheel when

you landed.'

Bertie surveyed the bike sadly. 'I'll have to walk,' he said. 'Where are we?'

Molly told him.

'But I'll never get home. It's miles.'

'I know,' said Molly. 'Wait here. Take your armour and clogs off for a minute.'

She came back when Bertie was bobbing against the ceiling again. She was pushing an old, black bike, just like his, with a basket on the front. But it had a little motor fixed to the rear wheel. 'Got this in China as well,' she said.

'But I can't ride that.'

'No, but I can. Here.' Molly handed him up a length of strong twine. 'Tie it round your tummy.'

Bertie made a really strong knot.

Molly tied the other end to the handlebars.

'Tight,' said Bertie.

'It won't slip,' she promised him, and she bundled the clogs up in the tin trousers and pushed them into the basket on the front of the bike.

'Right! Off we go!'

She played out the twine when they were outside, and let Bertie float up, high above the cottage. It was the first time he had actually allowed himself to float up, and, with the twine holding him fast to Molly's bike, he felt safe enough to enjoy it.

Molly's flat feet made her waddle like a duck

when she was walking, but her fat legs were strong and they were soon whizzing along.

'Hold your arms out,' she shouted up to him. 'Like a kite.'

Bertie spread his arms and it was like swimming in the air. He rose and fell, bobbed and dipped in the wind. And the twine tugged at his tummy and pulled him along behind the bike.

He loved it.

All those years he had carried all that fat, all that weight, he had never known what it was like to jump, or run without bouncing and wobbling, or dash about. He was still fat, he remembered, but he didn't weigh a thing.

Molly was a terrible cyclist, and several times Bertie wondered if he wouldn't end up being tugged behind an ambulance as he watched her ring her bell and shake her fist and even swear richly at motorists who had done nothing wrong except be in the part of the road she thought she should have.

'Crumbs,' he murmured. 'Get me home, safe, before you smash the bike.'

The fields and hedges, lanes and barns disappeared; and the rows of houses and shops, the little factories and offices told Bertie that they were getting near to home.

Children in a park stopped playing and looked up at Bertie as he glided over their heads.

'Look at that!'

'It's a balloon!'

'No, it's a kite, look!'

Fingers pointed and mouths gaped.

'Wow!'

Bertie kept his arms spread wide and his face quite still, so that no one should guess he was a real person.

It was growing dark when Molly found Bertie's house, and she was able to reel him in without anyone seeing.

Bertie gripped the handlebars of her bike to stop himself floating up again.

He was red-faced, breathless, and very happy. He had never known anything so wonderful as flying behind Molly's bike.

'Oh, thank you,' he said. 'Thank you.'

Gran opened the door. 'Bad news,' she said.

Chapter 10

Molly and Gran got on together right from the start.

Gran was grateful to Molly for looking after Bertie.

Molly liked Gran's sausage rolls.

They talked about Bertie as though he wasn't even there.

'He's always been fat,' said Gran.

'I don't mind,' said Molly. 'Fat doesn't bother me, but I can see that it's a bother when you're young.'

'When you're young,' agreed Gran.

'If you mind about it,' said Molly.

'He shouldn't mind,' said Gran.

'It's the same with ears,' said Molly.

'What do you mean?' said Gran.

Bertie listened, curious to know what fat had to do with ears.

'If they stick out,' said Molly, 'you'll get teased.'

'If you mind,' said Gran.

'That's it,' said Molly. 'Or big noses.'

'Or flat feet,' said Gran.

'Or speaking properly,' said Molly.

'Or not speaking properly,' said Gran.

'Or being too thin,' said Molly.

Bertie snorted. No one was too thin.

'If you mind,' said Gran.

'It's not what you look like,' said Molly, 'it's how you feel.'

'That's right,' said Gran. 'They don't tease you if you don't let them see you mind.'

'When I was a girl – ' began Molly. Bertie rolled his eyes in despair. Why did old people always talk about when they were girls, or boys? Old people had never been young, not really. It was all made up. 'When I was a girl,' said Molly, 'you could have hidden me behind a lamp-post I was so slim.'

Gran nodded.

Molly took another sausage roll.

'Seven stone, wet through,' said Molly. 'And dance! I could have danced till my shoes wore out. Oh. . .' She settled back in her chair and looked around, her pleasant smile painting her face with joy. 'Those were the days.'

'Now, Bertie,' explained Gran, 'wouldn't know what dancing is. Not that anyone dances these days. Not what I call dancing.'

'Not real dancing,' said Molly. And she pulled herself to her feet and spun round. Bertie just couldn't believe it. Molly danced around the room, and suddenly, her feet were not flat at all, but light and gay.

Gran clapped when Molly sat down again.

'You never forget,' said Gran.

'No. It's always there. Somewhere.'

Bertie looked down on them in disgust. He was sulking. That was another good thing about not weighing anything. You could just drift up to the ceiling, out of sight, and float there, above everything.

The bad news had been that Mr Platten had shut the pie shop for the rest of the week and gone on holiday. All of a sudden.

Gran had gone there to try to make him remember Mr Gupta. 'He was probably busy, when I asked,' said Gran. 'He'll remember.' But Pie Craft was locked and the blinds were pulled down, and there was a sign on the door saying: CLOSED – GONE ON HOLIDAY. So, that was that.

'I'm going to bed,' said Bertie. 'Thank you for bringing me back.'

Gran tied him to the mattress with his dressing-gown cord and shut the door quietly.

'You'll stay the night, won't you?' she said to Molly. 'It's very late.'

'I wouldn't mind,' said Molly.

The porridge got better. Next morning Bertie had three helpings of it, and a grapefruit, and toast.

He showed Gran the tin trousers and the clogs.

'You don't need to put on weight again,' she said.

76

'I can't wear these all the time,' he objected.

'You're welcome to keep them,' said Molly.

'That isn't the point,' he snapped.

'Bertie!' Gran warned him with her voice.

'Sorry,' said Bertie. 'But it isn't. I've got to find Mr Gupta's shop.'

'You can borrow my bike,' said Molly. 'Till yours is mended. I'll go home on the bus.'

'That's all right,' said Bertie. 'Look.'

He went out, and came back in a few minutes with his roller skates on.

'They're as good as clogs,' he said. 'With the tin trousers.'

'Good,' said Gran.

'Clever,' said Molly.

'And nearly as fast as the bike,' said Bertie.

Gran gave him a bag of sausage rolls, some sardine sandwiches, a flask of orange juice and an apple. He said goodbye to Molly. 'But I'll be back,' she warned, 'to see you and your gran.'

Bertie set off.

He sped along the pavement, still wobbling, but light as a feather. He went straight past the shop where he bought his chocolate, but he was so full after his breakfast that he didn't even look in the window.

He was having a good time. There was nearly a week to find Mr Gupta's. That should be long enough. And in the meantime, he was light, even if he was fat. And that was better than nothing. He pursed his lips, puffed out his cheeks and started to whistle.

The best plan was to go to the edge of where he knew the streets and then plunge into the area he didn't know. And he could draw a map, note down street names. That way, he'd start to get an idea of where he'd been, and he wouldn't go round and round in circles, through the strange streets.

He was pleased with himself. Happy. Hopeful.

Until he turned the corner, still whistling loudly, and saw Norman. And Norman's friends, throwing sticks up a tree at a cat.

'Here we go,' said Norman. 'A whistling pig.'

'Oink.'

'Oink.'

And they all laughed.

Bertie thought of Molly, and he tried not to mind. But he did mind. He skidded to a halt on the roller skates.

'Shut up,' he said.

Up in the tree, the cat miaowed pitifully. And Bertie stopped minding about them calling him names.

'You rotten bully,' said Bertie.

Norman's friends, who had been dancing around Bertie, grunting and squealing, suddenly stopped

and looked at him.

Norman flexed his fingers and made two fists.

'Say that again.'

Bertie looked at the silent group. He thought very quickly. Norman had never got him back for the ducking in the horse trough. Now that Bertie was standing still without his bike, he had no hope of beating Norman.

'He's scared,' one of the other boys taunted him.

'So he should be,' warned Norman, coming closer to Bertie.

Bertie had a brainwave. 'It's you that's scared,' he said.

Norman laughed. 'Scared of you, Porky?'

Bertie pointed to the cat. 'Scared to climb up and rescue him,' he said.

The cat miaowed. It was very high in the tree.

Norman snapped his knuckles.

'Not scared,' he said. 'Don't want to.'

Norman's gang looked on.

'But he could,' said a boy with a hair cut, 'if he wanted to.'

''Course he could,' they joined in. 'He could climb up there.'

Bertie smiled. 'Scared,' he said, softly.

Norman gave Bertie a punch. Not a hard one. Just to be going on with. Bertie gasped. 'Show me,' he said. His specs had misted up a bit. 'Show them.'

He pointed to Norman's gang.

Norman drew back his fist. This time it was going to be a really hard punch. And then there would be more. Bertie braced himself for the attack.

Chapter 11

Brrr. Brrrr.

Brrr. Brrrr.

Norman hesitated. He looked around.

'It's Porky!' shouted one of the gang. 'Hit him.'

Norman clenched his fist.

'Wait!' shouted Bertie.

'Well?'

'I'll climb the tree.'

They all laughed.

'You?'

'You'd break it.'

'Porky up a tree!'

Miaow.

Norman let his fist fall to his side. 'You wouldn't dare.'

Bertie looked up at the cat. It was a very long way up. 'You'll see,' he said.

Norman and his gang watched Bertie take off the roller boots. 'Can't climb in these,' he explained.

The gang jeered.

'He can't do it.'

'Hit him, Norm.'

'I will,' said Norman. 'Don't you worry.'

The second roller boot hit the pavement, and Bertie had to hold on to the tree to stop himself drifting up.

It was so easy. He just had to make sure that he held on tightly to a branch all the way up, changing hands as he went higher and higher, to stop himself from drifting right away.

Norman's gang watched in amazement.

Bertie reached the high branch and put his hand out to stroke the frightened cat.

'It's all right,' he said, softly. 'It's all right.'

The cat looked at him. Miaow.

'It's all right.' He stroked the soft black fur. 'Come on.'

'Coo-eee!' a voice shouted up.

Bertie looked down and saw a red, pie-shaped hat ride past on a bicycle.

'Coo-eee, fat boy!' Mr Gupta waved, put his hand back on the handlebars, rang his bell, and shot past.

'Stop!' called Bertie. 'Stop! I've got to talk to you.'

But Mr Gupta had gone.

The cat scrambled forward and threw itself into Bertie's arms. The extra weight was just enough to make Bertie float back down to earth. He took great care always to hold on to a branch, to make it look as though he was climbing down properly. When he was safely back on the pavement he cud-

dled the cat until he had his roller boots back on. Then he gave it a last stroke, the cat rubbed a rough tongue over his cheek and ran off.

Bertie stood up. 'I'll be off, then,' he said.

'Just a minute,' said Norman. 'You called me a bully.' He flexed his fist again.

'You are,' said Bertie. 'And a coward. You were frightened to climb the tree.'

'Wasn't.'

'Do it, then,' Bertie challenged him.

'The cat's down now,' jeered Norman.

'The tree's still there,' said Bertie. 'Climb it. I dare you.'

Norman's gang looked on. No one had ever spoken to Norman like this.

'Right. That's it,' said Norman. And he drew back his fist.

'Climb the tree,' said another boy.

'Climb it,' said another.

'Bertie did.'

'Go on.'

'Let's see you.'

Norman shrugged. 'Can't be bothered.'

'Leave him alone, then.'

'Well done, Bertie.'

'Thanks for getting the cat.'

Bertie didn't know what to do to the circle of friendly faces.

'Oh,' he said. 'Thank you.'

Bertie skated off. He looked back and saw the gang drift away, leaving Norman on his own. Bertie felt a strange, warm feeling. He waved and pushed on.

Brrr. Brrrr.

Brrr. Brrrr.

Now, he had to be quick. Mr Gupta was just ahead of him, on a bike. It wasn't so bad after all, this losing weight. Even if he was still fat.

Chapter 12

Bertie skated up the path and came to a halt at the front door.

'Any luck?' Gran asked.

'No.'

'You don't look too bothered.'

Bertie blinked at her. 'Don't I?'

'I'd have thought you'd be upset.'

'I looked everywhere,' said Bertie. 'There's no such road.'

'Vegetable lasagne,' said Gran.

Bertie managed to be more or less polite as he laid into the pasta and rich sauce, but he still got quite a lot on his chin.

'Lovely,' he said, putting out his bowl for more. 'It makes you hungry,' he said. 'On the skates.'

'It never used to,' said Gran. 'I've had your bike fixed.'

Bertie polished his bowl with a piece of garlic bread. He popped the bread into his mouth. 'Any more?'

'The road must be there. There's a Bakewell pudding.'

Bertie pulled a face. 'I'll try it,' he said.

Gran gave him a small piece. Then another, bigger one.

'These trousers,' began Bertie.

'Not with your mouth full,' said Gran.

Bertie swallowed. 'These trousers are too big,' he said.

Gran watched while Bertie pulled the waistband. It was certainly loose.

'I'll put a tuck in them,' she said.

Bertie washed up the dishes while Gran got her sewing things out.

'I'd have thought you'd be upset,' she said. 'Not finding that Mr Gupta.'

Bertie told her about Norman and the cat. 'And the others,' he finished. 'They looked at me like . . .'

'Yes?'

'Like . . .'

'Go on.' Her needle flashed.

'Like they might let me be their friend.'

'Why not?'

Bertie dried a pudding bowl. 'I'm so fat,' he said.

'Doesn't matter.'

Bertie flicked a blob of soap suds from his nose.

'And you're not as fat as you were. Look at these.' Gran held up the trousers and showed him the big tuck she had taken in.

Bertie skated over to her.

'But I'm eating masses,' he said.

'Good food, though.'

Bertie took the trousers, skated to the door, took off the roller boots and floated upstairs. He was getting good at this.

He tied himself to his bed with his dressing-gown cord and hovered, thinking. When the picture of the friendly faces of Norman's gang came into his mind, he smiled, and it made him shiver a little with pleasure. He reached out and took a bar of chocolate from his special store. He unwrapped it and put it to his mouth. He always munched chocolate when he was thinking. He nibbled a tiny piece off the edge, let it melt in his mouth, then he swallowed. He pulled a face, wrapped the rest of the bar back up again and put it away.

After another big breakfast of porridge and toast Bertie clanked his bike along the path and waved to Gran.

The Chinese tin trousers were quite comfortable now. Bertie still wobbled a bit when the bicycle clanked along, but not as much as before.

He pedalled along, his feet clumsy in the roller boots, but his cheeks glowing with happiness. Today, he would find the street. He just knew he would.

Norman scowled at him as he rattled past.

'Brrr. Brrrr,' trilled Bertie. 'Going for a climb?'

Norman clenched his fists but he said nothing.

Bertie swerved round the corner and down the road.

Norman's gang waved to Bertie. He took one hand off the handlebars and waved back.

'Miaow!' Dave shouted.

Bertie grinned. It was better than OINK! But, come to think of it, he wouldn't mind OINK so much today. Not if Dave smiled at him when he said it.

He pushed down on the pedals and enjoyed the sensation of spinning along, past the shops, through the park, down the hill and into the lower part of town where he knew Mr Gupta had his shop.

There was the gas holder. Bertie remembered that. Then the floodlights on the football ground. Good. And wasn't that old cinema familiar? Yes!

Bertie pumped furiously at the pedals. It was right! He was there! Round the next corner, and, YES! This was the road. He had found it. Count the numbers. One. Three. Five. HELP! HELP! Seven. HELP! What?

Number eleven. And three faces leaned out. A woman and two children. 'HELP!'

A dark stream of smoke flowed out under the front door.

Bertie jammed on his brakes and screeched to a halt.

'Oh, thank goodness. Help! Please help!' the

woman shouted down to Bertie.

'What shall I do?'

'Ring the fire brigade.'

Bertie gulped. Brrr. Brrrr.

This was no good.

'What's happening?' asked a man with a cap.

'Oh, look,' said a lady with a small dog.

'They're stuck,' said a man with a pipe.

'I'll ring,' said a woman in overalls.

The woman in the high window shouted louder. The two children cried.

'They're on their way,' said the woman in overalls.

'It might be too late,' said the man with the pipe.

'The stairs are on fire,' shouted the woman. 'We can't get out. Oh, please help.'

'They're on their way,' said the woman in overalls again.

Smoke poured out of the upper window. The woman coughed. 'I'm throwing the children down!' she shouted. 'Catch them!'

'No! It's too high!'

Bertie looked round. There was no fire engine.

'Wait!' he called. 'I'll come and get them.'

The man with the pipe laughed. Not a nice laugh.

Bertie unfastened himself from his bike. He floated a little above the ground. He took off the roller boots and dropped them.

He floated up, slowly.

The crowd gasped.

As he rose, Bertie travelled faster. He was going at quite a rate when he reached the window. He stretched out a hand and grabbed the sill. The woman stared at him in amazement.

'Wait here,' said Bertie. 'I'll only be a minute. Give me the children.'

A little girl climbed out of the window and held on tight to Bertie, like a monkey. A little boy followed. Bertie took him and slowly floated back down to earth.

Then he floated back up.

'Come on,' he said to the woman.

'I can't. We'll fall.'

The smoke was thick and black, making Bertie's eyes water. 'It's all right. Come on.'

'I can't.'

Flames snatched greedily into the room. There was a crackling and a roaring. Bertie grabbed her. He hauled her out and she clung to him.

They drifted down, coming to a rest with a thump on the pavement.

'Oh!' gasped the woman. She let go of Bertie and he floated away.

'Catch me!' he shouted.

The man with the pipe snatched him. 'Gotcher!'

'The boots,' said Bertie.

He put them on and floated an inch above

the pavement.

Hee-haw. Hee-haw. Hee-haw. The fire engine veered round the corner.

'They're all out,' said a man.

The woman cuddled the children and thanked Bertie, but he could hardly hear. The woman with the overalls hoisted him up on to her shoulders.

'You're light,' she said.

They all laughed.

The firemen rolled out their hoses and started to douse the fire.

The crowd carried Bertie, shoulder high, down the road. They cheered and roared.

Bertie was breathless with embarrassment and pride.

'Hooray!'

Mr Gupta peered out of his shop window as Bertie was carried past.

'Stop!' shouted Bertie. 'Let me down! Let me down! I've got to speak to him!'

But his words were lost in the cheering and he was carried past. Mr Gupta raised his hands above his head in salute to the triumphant Bertie. And behind him, wasn't that? Surely it was the dim figure of Mr Platten? Bertie was swept past.

'Oh, stop!' he cried. 'Please stop!'

'Hooray! Hooray!'

They carried him through the streets, past the gas

holder, through the park, cheering all the way.

Hee-haw. Hee-haw. Hee-haw.

The fire engine came up to the parade.

'Are you the lad?' shouted the Chief.

'That's him!'

'He's the one.'

Bertie caught sight of Norman's face in the crowd that had gathered.

'Well done,' said the Fire Chief. 'You're very brave.'

He hauled Bertie off the shoulders of the crowd and into the fire engine.

They cheered even louder.

The man with the pipe pushed Bertie's bike up on to the back of the fire engine. Willing hands made it safe.

Hee-haw. Hee-haw. The fire engine made a circuit of honour round the park as the huge crowd cheered and cheered and Bertie waved.

'Take me back,' he begged, as the procession finished. 'Take me back to the fire.'

But they drove him to the fire station, gave him a proper helmet and a pair of firemen's trousers. Then they took him home.

His gran was so proud of him.

'But I'll never find the street again,' groaned Bertie when it was all quiet and they were on their own.

'You will,' said Gran.

But he didn't. Not the next day, nor the next, even though he looked very hard.

Chapter 13

Every day Bertie cycled round the town, but he never found Mr Gupta's shop again.

Every night Gran secretly put another tuck in the waistband of his trousers.

On Sunday, the last day of the holiday, Bertie pedalled sadly to Mr Platten's shop. He leaned the bike against the doorway and peered through the window. Nothing. No one. Empty.

A sign in the door said: OPEN TOMORROW. So, Mr Platten had been in, but he was nowhere to be seen.

The long, last day stretched out in front of Bertie. School tomorrow. And how could he go round in Chinese tin trousers and a pair of roller boots? They'd never let him.

'Hey, Bertie!'

It was Dave, from Norman's gang.

'Coming? We're going to the park.'

Bertie had never been invited anywhere before. 'You don't want me,' he said.

'Come on, there's balloons.'

'No, I'm not bothered.'

'Big ones,' said Pete. 'Real ones. With baskets

with people in them.'

Bertie hesitated.

'Look,' said Dave. 'We're sorry.'

'Yes,' Pete agreed.

'You know. About, well – Porky, and things.'

'Yes.'

Bertie looked round for Norman.

'He's not with us,' said Pete. 'We don't go with him any more.'

'Why not?'

'Because of climbing the tree.'

'He was scared.'

'You weren't.'

'I was,' said Bertie.

'But you climbed it.'

'Sort of.'

'Come on,' said Dave.

'I've got a kite,' said Pete. 'Look.'

Bertie gave in. 'All right.'

'Great!'

'Hey,' said Dave.

'What?'

'You're thin.'

They looked at Bertie.

'No, he's not,' said Pete.

'Well, no,' said Dave. 'Not thin. But not fat.'

'Not as fat as he was,' said Pete.

'Not fat at all, really,' said Dave.

'I've been eating different food,' said Bertie.

'Come on,' said Pete. 'We'll miss it.'

They cycled together to the park.

Bertie gasped.

The balloons were huge.

'Wow!' said Pete.

'That's amazing.'

The whole sky was full of balloons.

There were full, round ones, like onions. But the best ones were shaped like all sorts of things.

There was a green, Chinese dragon, with four legs and red flames streaming out of its mouth. 'Coo-ee! Bertie!' Molly waved down from the dragon basket.

There was a pie, with crinkled edges. 'Bertie. Hello.' Mr Platten waved down. 'Great fun. Wurr. Wurrrr.'

Bertie bounced up and down in excitement. 'Come down! I've got to speak to you.'

'Wurrrr. Wurr,' laughed Mr Platten.

A red hat balloon, with gold trimming, floated over Bertie's head. 'Hello, there!' called Mr Gupta.

'Stop! Stop! I've got to talk to you!'

'Where's that fat boy?' shouted Mr Gupta, pointing at Bertie.

'He got thin,' shouted Dave. 'Well, thinner.'

Pete looked sadly at his kite. 'I won't be able to fly this,' he said. 'It'll catch up in the balloons.'

'I wish we could go up,' said Dave.

'Boo!' called Norman. 'Oink! Oink!'

Bertie looked round, face pale with anger, fists clenched.

'Yah! Boo!' Norman drifted past in a balloon shaped like a pig.

'Clear out,' shouted Dave.

'Boys. Boys,' said Mr Formalyn as he drifted overhead in a giant telephone.

'Brrr. Brrrr.'

'Oh, you can't fool me, Bertie George. I've worked out your game.'

Bertie's cheeks went red.

'Never mind, Bertie,' said Gran. 'You won't be in fights now. You've got your new friends.' She grinned down at them from an inflated hat with a bunch of grapes, and a bird with yellow and blue feathers.

'I wish we could . . .' began Pete, but there was a scream, then a gasp from the crowd.

Norman had lost control of the balloon when he shouted down to the boys, and he was blowing towards the gas holder.

'Go higher,' called Mr Formalyn. 'More hot air.'

But it was too late. Norman was heading straight for the giant container.

'He'll explode if he hits it,' said Dave. 'With his burner.'

'Stand round me,' said Bertie. The boys surrounded him while he slipped off his roller boots, then his trousers, then the tin trousers underneath.

'Better put these back on,' he said, slipping his trousers back.

He tied the twine from Pete's kite tight around his waist.

'Get hold of it,' he said.

He dropped the boots and the tin trousers. As soon as the weight was gone he flew up into the air, much faster than he had when he had saved the people from the fire.

Pete and Dave and the others dug their heels in the soft grass to stop themselves from being tugged after him.

They played the twine out, controlling him, drawing him towards the balloon with Norman in.

He swept past Mr Gupta. 'I want to talk to you,' he said.

'Any time, thin boy. Any time.'

Norman was shouting and waving his arms. The balloon-pig was racing towards the gas holder. Its hot air burners threw out red flames in a desperate, hopeless attempt to gain height.

Bertie reached out, grabbed Norman's hand, and he tugged hard, pulling him clear.

Norman dangled, slipped, nearly dropped. The crowd gasped. People hid their eyes.

Bertie felt the twine tug at his waist. He grabbed

101

again, caught Norman, held him tight. He had got him.

'Ooh!' gasped the crowd. The twine pulled them down, swiftly. The balloon lurched up, free from Norman's weight, and sailed just over the top of the gas holder.

'Ahh!' gasped the crowd.

'Pull me in,' shouted Bertie.

Dave and Pete dragged at the twine.

'Oh, help,' whimpered Norman. 'Help. Get me down.' He screwed his eyes up tight.

The balloonists clapped and cheered. They tugged the ropes on their balloons and let out the hot air.

Bertie landed with a thump.

Norman twisted his ankle when he hit the ground.

The balloons circled round, losing height.

Norman cried.

Bertie pulled his tin trousers on over his proper ones.

'You look stupid,' sniffed Norman.

'But not fat,' said Mr Gupta, tying up his balloon.

'Wurrrr. Wurrrr,' Mr Platten laughed. 'But not fat, eh? Solid.' He poked Bertie, who was still sort of chunky. 'But not fat.'

His pie-balloon bobbed in the air, the rope twanging in the breeze.

Bertie looked at himself in wonder.

'You're right,' he said.

'You hadn't noticed,' said Gran.

'All week,' said Dave, 'we saw you, pedalling round.'

Bertie grinned happily.

'I sewed your trousers,' said Gran.

Bertie's cheeks wobbled with pleasure, for they had hardly lost their roundness at all. They were like a reminder of what he had been.

'I'm not fat,' said Bertie. 'I'm really not.'

'Good food,' said Gran.

'Good pies,' said Mr Platten. 'Wurrrr. Wurrrr.'

'That's right,' said Bertie. 'I eat more now than ever. I need it, the way I've been riding round.'

'Have some chocolate,' Mr Gupta offered.

'No thanks. I don't eat it.'

'But you'll have a pie,' said Mr Platten.

A van drew up with a little funnel on the roof and a delicious scent of filled pastry. The driver jumped out, flung open the back doors and set up a stall.

PIE CRAFT

'What's going on?' asked Bertie.

'Business expanding,' said Mr Platten. 'Dial-a-Pie.'

'Or a samosa,' said Mr Gupta.

'I want a word with you,' said Bertie.

104

Chapter 14

Norman had dried his eyes and was tucking into a lentil and aubergine pie when Bertie George and Mr Gupta left the park. Bertie's bike whirred and clanked alongside them as they walked through the small streets.

'Can you make me heavy again?' asked Bertie.

'Fat?'

'You didn't make me thin,' said Bertie.

'That's true.'

They turned another corner, and there was the street.

'Why couldn't I find it?' asked Bertie.

'It's a funny thing, memory,' said Mr Gupta. And his eyes twinkled.

Two children rushed up to Bertie and hugged him.

'See our door,' they said.

And they showed him a brightly painted front door and a house full of flowers.

'Oh,' said a lady. 'People were so kind after the fire. See how they've cleared up the mess.'

'That's lovely,' said Bertie. 'I'm glad.'

Something sharp dug into his back.

'You were fat,' said a man waving a pipe at Bertie.

'Well, I'm not now.'

'Thank you,' said the lady. 'I don't know how you saved us, but thank you.'

'No, you're not,' said the man with the pipe. 'You're still stocky, though.'

'I'll settle for that,' said Bertie.

'Here,' said the lady, handing Bertie a big box of chocolates.

Bertie thanked her and put them in the basket of his bike. For his gran.

The bell jangled as they went into Mr Gupta's shop.

Bertie took off the tin trousers and the roller boots and floated up to take a closer look at the crocodile.

'It's a bit dusty,' he said.

Mr Gupta threw a yellow duster up to him.

'I can never reach,' he said. 'You do it. Now, where did I put that stuff?'

He looked in cupboards, under the counter, even in the till.

'Tell me,' said Bertie.

'Yes.'

'You knew all the time, didn't you?'

'Knew what?'

'About me.'

'How could I?'

Bertie ran the duster over the crocodile's back, feeling the bumpy ridges. 'Mr Platten told you,' he said.

'Where's that remedy?' asked Mr Gupta.

'What is the truth about Pie Craft?' asked Bertie.

'Ah.'

'Well?'

'Got it.'

Mr Gupta held up a small bottle.

Bertie hauled himself down the shelves.

'Will it make me heavy?'

'Yes.'

'Well, what is the truth?'

Mr Gupta smiled. 'I have known Mr Platten a long time,' he said.

'I thought so.'

'He sometimes borrows things from me. Remedies. He puts them into pies.'

'Wow.'

'For special people.'

'Why didn't he put it in mine?'

'I haven't got a remedy for fatness.'

'So?'

'So we had to think of a plan. You had to eat good food to make yourself heavy. No more chocolate or chips. Good food. And you had to take lots of exercise.'

'So he went on holiday?'

Mr Gupta smiled. 'Would you like the heavy remedy?'

Bertie took the bottle.

'I like floating,' he said. 'Now that I'm not fat.'

'Drink.'

Bertie took out the stopper and sniffed it. He lifted it to his lips.

'Drink,' said Mr Gupta.

Bertie looked round the shop, at the bottles and jars and packets.

'Are all these remedies?'

'Oh, yes.'

'Do they all work?'

'Of course.'

Bertie looked at the small bottle in his hand. He hesitated.

'What do they do?' he asked.

'Are you going to take that remedy?' asked Mr Gupta.

'I might,' said Bertie. 'Or another one.'

The Weekly Ghost

by Toby Forward

'. . . there was something in it about a girl called Sara, who walks around the school at night.'
'A real girl?' asked Stephanie.
'No,' said Joey. 'A school ghost.'

When Stephanie and her friends start *The Weekly Post*, they are astonished to find that a front page story in the first edition has been changed overnight to a shocking new story. Even more strangely, the paper's name has been changed to *The Weekly Ghost*. Who has been tampering with their newspaper?

This unusual ghost story comes from the author of the widely acclaimed *Wyvern* Quartet.

READ MORE IN PUFFIN

For children of all ages, Puffin represents quality and variety – the very best in publishing today around the world.

For complete information about books available from Puffin – and Penguin – and how to order them, contact us at the appropriate address below. Please note that for copyright reasons the selection of books varies from country to country.

On the world wide web: www.penguin.co.uk

In the United Kingdom: Please write to *Dept. EP, Penguin Books Ltd, Bath Road, Harmondsworth, West Drayton, Middlesex UB7 0DA*

In the United States: Please write to *Consumer Sales, Penguin USA, P.O. Box 999, Dept. 17109, Bergenfield, New Jersey 07621-0120.* VISA and MasterCard holders call 1-800-253-6476 to order Penguin titles

In Canada: Please write to *Penguin Books Canada Ltd, 10 Alcorn Avenue, Suite 300, Toronto, Ontario M4V 3B2*

In Australia: Please write to *Penguin Books Australia Ltd, P.O. Box 257, Ringwood, Victoria 3134*

In New Zealand: Please write to *Penguin Books (NZ) Ltd, Private Bag 102902, North Shore Mail Centre, Auckland 10*

In India: Please write to *Penguin Books India Pvt Ltd, 706 Eros Apartments, 56 Nehru Place, New Delhi 110 019*

In the Netherlands: Please write to *Penguin Books Netherlands bv, Postbus 3507, NL-1001 AH Amsterdam*

In Germany: Please write to *Penguin Books Deutschland GmbH, Metzlerstrasse 26, 60594 Frankfurt am Main*

In Spain: Please write to *Penguin Books S. A., Bravo Murillo 19, 1° B, 28015 Madrid*

In Italy: Please write to *Penguin Italia s.r.l., Via Felice Casati 20, I–20124 Milano*

In France: Please write to *Penguin France S. A., 17 rue Lejeune, F–31000 Toulouse*

In Japan: Please write to *Penguin Books Japan, Ishikiribashi Building, 2–5–4, Suido, Bunkyo-ku, Tokyo 112*

In South Africa: Please write to *Longman Penguin Southern Africa (Pty) Ltd, Private Bag X08, Bertsham 2013*